The Boy Who Kicked Pigs

Born a Catholic in Irish Liverpool in 1934, Tom Baker tried being a monk, a sailor and a builder's labourer before settling for a career on the stage. From a struggling start he went on to appear at the National Theatre, to work with Pasolini, to Hollywood, and finally to star as the ultimate Doctor Who.

D1099955

The Boy
Who Kicked Pigs

TOM BAKER

illustrated by David Roberts

ff

faber and faber

for my wife Sue Jerrard

Illustrations by David Roberts,
who dedicates this work to Lynn

First published in 1999
by Faber & Faber Limited
3 Queen Square WC1N 3AU

This editon first published in 2006
by Faber and Faber limited

Typeset by Faber & Faber Ltd
Printed in England by CPI Bookmarque, Croydon

A CIP record for this book
is available from the British Library

ISBN 978–0–571–23054–9
ISBN 0–571–23054–7

4 6 8 10 9 7 5 3

The Boy
Who Kicked Pigs

Robert having an evil thought.

Saturday, June the 13th. And Robert Caligari is going to die today. It's a marvellous day. The place is Sandway in Kent, near Lenham, the highest village in the county. It is 7.30 in the morning. It is the sort of day that makes you glad to be alive and it is a Saturday too. To be young on a warm sunny Saturday in June is simply wonderful. And today is the day Robert Caligari is going to die.

He is thirteen years old and has lived all his life in Lenham village. Four thousand, seven hundred and forty-five days he has spent in the same little village, and today, on June 13th, he is going to die. He doesn't know; not yet, anyway.

This really is a very sad and terrible story. It is a tale of undiluted horror. This is the story of a boy who is considered to be a monster. The people who are supposed to know about these things, adults, said afterwards that

'He's beyond the pale.'

he was beyond the pale. That's the sort of thing that grown ups often say when they don't really know what they are talking about. 'He's beyond the pale,' they say. But you can make up your own mind when you have found out something about Robert Caligari for yourself.

When I began to write this story I asked a few grown up people to look at a draft. Do you know what they said about it? Go on, have a guess. You're right! You've got it in one! They said: Whoever writes stuff like this is beyond the pale, he's sick. That's what they said. Anyway, I don't much care what they said. The story happened and I have to write it down, so there. And if you decide to read the story, then good luck to you, I say. You can decide for yourself. And if you like it then you can tell me about it, even though some adults might consider you odd in the head. And if you don't like it then some grown-ups will be pleased because they'll think you're on their side.

While we are on this point of who agrees with whom I'll give you a tip. This tip is well meant so don't get all upset. It's just between you and me. It's a tip that spells power, like the tip of a wand, if you know what I mean.

'Turned out nice, officer.'

It's simply this: whenever you have anything, repeat, *anything* to do with authority in any form, always be polite. No, no, hold on, hold on. I don't mean crawling, especially I don't mean crawling. I mean just be polite and smile a little. Why? Because it does their heads in, that's why. If you can bring yourself to do this you will discover that you have the power to get pretty well whatever you want out of people. Look, if someone told you that it's a good idea not to go through a red traffic light you'd think they were thick, it's so obvious. But obvious as it is, the advice would be true, right? The same with calm, good-natured politeness. I say good-natured because there is, of course, a sly, smiling, sarcastic sort of politeness that isn't politeness at all. You'll often see it in films or on television. And on the telly it always gets a laugh and seems very clever. But in real life it hardly ever works and always makes people hate you. In fact it often leads to a punch-up and sometimes even to somebody getting killed. Politeness is a form of language and an attitude that yields real high profit for a young person. It gives you almost magical powers. In

Robert guzzling the small ads.

its own way it's as powerful as money. It can buy people's co-operation. And it's nice having power over people. Anyone who says it isn't nice is just talking balls. Try it for a few minutes and you will agree as you feel the pleasure of power.

Now let's get on with this terrible tale.

Robert Caligari was a great reader of the local paper. It was called the *Kent Clarion*. He didn't read the main stories, of course. Usually, they are so amazingly boring you might fall into a coma if you read more than, say, two of them within thirty minutes. Local papers are dull and even dangerous too. In fact, if you ever find a friend of yours in a deep state of unconsciousness, the first thing to do is check to see if your friend has been reading the local paper. If he or she has, then throw the paper out of the window and let as much fresh air into the room as possible and make a cup of sweet hot tea for your friend. With a bit of luck you might save a life.

No, Robert Caligari knew better than to read the main stories. He preferred the classified ads. He looked at them very carefully because they gave him a good

Robert as a little devil with two-thirds of his mother.

picture of the inside of people's minds. The classified ads, even when they're naff, are always more interesting than the so-called main stories. Classified ads tell you, sometimes in a coded way, what people are really thinking about. The small ads meant a lot to Robert and fed his vivid imagination. No, vivid is not quite the word to describe his imagination. Greedy would be more exact; or perhaps very greedy. No. Got it! It's not vivid or greedy, the word is *insatiable*. That's it, insatiable. That means 'cannot be satisfied'. And that's the way it was inside Robert's head. His imagination could not be satisfied. When he became interested in something then he could not get enough of it. There are quite a lot of people like that around the place. Some are fascinated by music and know everything there is to know about pop groups. Others are like that about football teams, or soap operas. They just can't get enough of what revs them up. It's called Trivial Pursuits by sarcastic adults.

When Robert was a small boy his mother noticed that in some respects he was a bit odd. I'll give you an example. His sister Nerys is about two years older than

Thrifty Nerys feeds her pet pig Trevor.

Robert and has a little lump on her bottom lip, the result of falling against the kitchen wall while playing her recorder. This Nerys was a thrifty girl, always popping pennies in her piggy bank when she was young. She's still thrifty, only now she pops pounds. When Robert was just a nipper she was always rattling her little tin pig, especially if there were visitors to the house, know what I mean? She called this tin pig Trevor. And she would shake him quite loudly when some visitor was there and she would say things like, 'Oh, I think Trevor's a bit hungry today, his tummy sounds empty.' Oh, little Nerys had the makings of a miser. Anyway, she was always rattling her pig and trying to guess how much money there might be in its belly. Robert didn't like this little pig. In fact he hated Nerys's little pig, and he longed to take it to market. Know what I mean? And whenever Nerys wasn't looking Robert would kick this little tin pig. He would set Trevor up in the middle of the sitting room with a little cushion under his bottom, to protect his foot (Robert's foot, that is). And then he would back away, and just like a Kiwi kicker he would rush at the pig and boot it

Trevor the pig on the telly.

across the room. The first couple of hundred times he did it were quite funny for the people who saw it, except for Nerys of course. She used to make an awful scene about her little pig getting Robert's boot up its arse. And so she would hide her little pig for his own safety. But she couldn't stop Robert from finding and kicking her tiny, tinny Trevor. There was some trouble in the house once when Robert kicked the pig so hard that it flew (oh yes, pigs can fly, if you kick them hard enough). Across the room flew little tin Trevor and bang! He went straight through the television screen and half way up the tube at the back. *Postman Pat* was on at the time and was Nerys mad? Yes, she was. After that little incident kicking pigs in the direction of the television set was forbidden.

For a few days all went well. The telly was replaced and life became bearable again at number 7a Vampire Close. Funny name for a street. It was named after a nice little man called Boris who had come to live in the district just after the Second World War. He was a dotty little chap with a odd way of talking and a funny way of walking and his left ear lobe dangled down nearly as

Boris of Transylvanian Bats.

low as his shirt collar. He used to tell Robert and his pals that his schoolmaster back home had a habit of pulling boys' ear lobes. To the children in the village Boris seemed quite old. Except of course when he was standing next to the church, which dated back to the thirteenth century, and then he looked quite young. But then most people look young in an old churchyard. But Boris was nice, and that's the important thing, don't you think? He became mad keen on cricket, did Boris, and went to all the Kent home games and attended the local amateur games too. And if old Mr Killick the regular scorer ever failed to turn up, and he did fail sometimes as he was a bottle-nosed old stumbler, then Boris would stand in and take the score book. Boris became so obsessed with cricket he even started up a small business in his garden shed where he made cricket bats to his own design which he exported to Transylvania, where he came from. It became quite a thriving little enterprise. He called it 'Transylvanian Bats Ltd'.

When old Boris died he left all his money to the local village. There was a small housing development just

Trevor teed-up on an egg-cup.

being completed at the time of his death and as a token of respect and gratitude the local council called this new bit of the village Vampire Close. As it was quite near the church, the churchwarden made a bit of a fuss and pungent remarks about garlic and so on; but all to no avail, and Vampire Close kept its name.

One day, it was in the summer, Robert was alone in the front room watching *Postman Pat* again and suddenly he was struck with the desire to kick a pig. His toes tingled and itched and his calf muscles fluttered. Robert was possessed. He opened the door and peeped around in case the dreaded Nerys was about the place. No sign of her and no sound of muttering from his mother in the kitchen. Robert nipped along to Nerys's bedroom and fetched her pig Trevor, which she kept hidden in an antique chamber pot on top of her wardrobe. Nothing escaped Robert. He stood the pig on a wooden egg-cup, its snout towards the open window. It was a lovely warm day and conditions for kicking a pig were just perfect. Robert tucked a cushion under Trevors rump, retreated four paces and psyched himself up. There was a breathless hush in Vampire Close as

Bye-bye Trevor. Hello chaos.

Robert withdrew into himself in preparation for the kick of a lifetime. And then he burst into life and delivered a marvellous kick to Trevor's arse. Again the pig flew. Out through the open window he went like an Exocet missile.

A police car with its window wound down was cruising past the house at the very moment that Robert did his pig trick. The little tin creature carrying about two pounds and sixty pence in small coins in its stomach sailed through the cop car window. The driver, a PC by the name of George Weller, had just received an order from headquarters to rush to the scene of a suspected robbery; a violin was thought to have been nicked. He gunned the engine, and just as he screamed off in first gear Trevor the flying pig came in through the open window and butted PC Weller in the temple. The pig kiss blacked out the policeman's brain, and he swerved hard right and crashed into a parked fish van, a wet-fish van with the words 'Best Plaice Mobile Fish' painted on the side.

Chaos! Flukes flew all over the the floor. A nosy woman aged about forty-six with a patch over her left eye jumped

A copper off his trolley after being kissed by a pig.

sideways to avoid the flying flukes. She dropped her shopping bag on to the pavement and out fell her bananas, seven of them, a bottle of Camp coffee essence and a very large bone, the sort of bone any dog worth his salt would die for. PC Weller staggered out of his car and approached the fishmonger to see if all was well. He was walking with both hands out in front of him because he couldn't see very well after being kissed on the head by a flying pig. The poor fishman, whose glasses had been broken in the crash, was absolutely gutted. He was busy groping for his flukes. The constable approached at an angle, wondering how he could blame the whole little incident on the fishmonger. Dazed as he was, he did not perceive the bananas on the pavement in front of him. 'Hello, hello, hello,' he cried as he drew near the fluke collector. 'What's going on . . .?' And as the fishman turned to say hello to whoever had just said hello three times to him, the haddock-footed policeman trod on the seven bananas.

To tread on one banana can be quite serious, as anyone who has ever read the autobiography of Will Fyffe will tell you. But to tread on seven is really chancing

Poins the bull terrier and his mistress.

your arm a bit and can be deadly. The policeman's name was George, remember. And just by George as he skidded on the seven deadly bananas was a very bad-tempered-looking bull terrier, dirty white in colour and with a black patch over his right eye. As George the policeman hit the pavement with a very interesting thud, he threw out his left arm, grasping at straws, to save himself. Too late. All that came to hand was the big bone. Without realizing what he was doing, George raised his left hand towards his head. The bull terrier, whose name was Poins, thought that George the policeman was going to have his bone away (Poins's bone, that is). Poins had been badly abused as a pup in Muswell Hill, London N10, and he wasn't going to stand by and watch some skidding copper snaffle his bone. In a flash Poins was in, like Flynn. He bit the beached PC in his right buttock and seized his back bone; I mean bone back. Then, in his eagerness to hold on to his property, Poins the dog leaped into the fish van to be alone with his bone. The flukemonger screamed in horror at the sight of a dirty white bull terrier in among his cod fillets. Poins growled ferociously and backed further off and

Poins in the scampi tray.

got his dirty bum comfortable in a tray of scampi. The forty-six-year-old lady with the eye patch, who turned out to be Poins's mistress, though most people thought she was his sister, rushed forward to protect her terrier. She didn't notice the seven banana skins that PC George had trodden on and which actually belonged to her. What a mistake. What a mistake! And did she go a purler? She did indeed. And she flew – no, that's not the word – she ricocheted (that's the only word) like a bullet off a marble slab and under the fish wagon she went. Whoosh! Crump! Everybody heard the loud click as her ankle snapped as clean as a bishop's crozier in a dragon's mouth. Or as clean as a whistle. If you know what I mean.

Young Robert Caligari watched all this uproar with a very wide smile on his little face. Just then his sister Nerys rushed into their sitting-room carrying an empty chamber pot in her left hand and demanded to know where Trevor was. Robert pointed towards the scene outside the window. 'He's been arrested,' he said. 'Look, the police have got him.' By now the policeman was upright. An ambulance had arrived as well as another police car, and the

The villagers enjoy catastrophe in the High Street.

concussed copper, George, was holding up the little tin pig as he tried to explain how the whole uproar had started.

'But pigs don't fly,' the newly arrived sergeant said ponderously. He was a fan of John Thaw so he said everything ponderously and with a touch of mystery as if he was the Oracle at Delphi. 'Well, this little bleeder flew,' shrieked George, 'as true as my name's Arthur.' The sergeant, knowing that Arthur was not George's name, deduced instantly that his colleague was either up to no good, or was concussed, or had just vacated his mind, which is very common with stressed coppers. That's why they retire so quick when things go wrong.

A small group of innocent passers-by were happily splitting their sides with laughter and stamping their feet to ease the cramps. One of the spectators, an ex-xylophone player who had lost his nerve and now did meals-on-wheels, suddenly recovered his old confidence and mimed his old instrument joyously. The coppers went potty. There are very few things in life as pleasurable as seeing a demented British copper going off his trolley, and we all know that policemen don't like to see anybody laughing; in fact it is well known that

Robert kicks a woman in the pork chops.

policemen and doctors are both very anti-pleasure. This whole scene pleased Robert quite a bit, and he decided that he would kick pigs more often if that's all it took to make people laugh.

And so it went on for years. Robert simply could not pass a pig without kicking it. Once at an agricultural show he rushed into the ring where some prize pigs were being judged and in front of nearly eighteen hundred astonished spectators he kicked the supreme champion pig of all England, an Essex Blackleg. There was such booing from the bacon-crazed crowd that even Robert was a bit daunted. After that he didn't kick a pig for yonks.

But one day a couple of years later when he and his mother were passing the local butcher's shop, 'Tod Slaughter, Butcher and Grazier', Robert noticed a lady buy thirteen pork chops for her weekend dinner. She was a huge woman who lived alone in a nearby council house. She had a husband but as his wife grew large on pork chops, the husband had to leave home and find a room down in the village. He was still quite fond of his wife and could often be seen talking to her through the window of her council house; there wasn't room for him to go in. Anyway,

Dr Porter tries to find Robert's heart.

as this poor woman about the size of a chapel passed Robert and his mother she said, 'Good afternoon, Mrs Caligari', and to Robert she said: 'And how is Robert today?' In answer to which Robert kicked her in the pork chops.

Robert's mother was so embarrassed she didn't know what to do. She spoke to their doctor about Robert and his passion for kicking pigs or pork, whichever was nearer. Dr Porter, who was a vegetarian and hadn't seen a pork chop since the Festival of Britain, was baffled too. 'Perhaps he'll grow out of it,' he said. And then just as suddenly as it had started it stopped again.

It happened like this. One day Robert was in the local café, The Glade it was called. He was buying himself a Lion Bar and he suddenly noticed a bacon sandwich sitting all by itself on a plate at a discreet table in the corner of the café. It did not appear to have an owner. Robert assumed that the sandwich was unwanted, an orphan sandwich, so to speak. And where Robert Caligari was concerned, orphan sandwiches got no mercy. Robert suddenly wanted to kick the innocent sandwich out of the café and into the great wide world outside. But the sandwich was not an orphan. The man who owned the

The fatal bacon butty sails to its final resting place.

sandwich, and who loved it too, just happened to be getting himself a second mug of tea at the counter. When he saw Robert kidnap his precious bacon butty and run to the door of the café and attempt a drop kick with it, well, he just lost his head and saw red. As Robert watched the hijacked butty sail over the cemetery wall outside the café he heard a terrible roar, like the sound of a bereaved elephant, and he suddenly felt himself seized by the scruff of his neck and the seat of his jeans and, just like Trevor the pig all those years before, Robert flew over the church wall hot in the same trajectory as the mugged butty. He fell headlong into what felt like a scalding pond of stinging nettles. A neglected grave carrying the name Cheesemans and suggesting, rather improbably, that the aforesaid Cheesemans was merely sleeping, nestled in the nettles where the kidnapped and abused butty had landed. The headstone of the sleeping Mr Cheesemans caught Robert a glancing blow to his medulla oblongata or whatever the right side of the brain is called, and hey presto, the butty mugger was cured of his desire to abuse bacon. It's a funny old world, isn't it?

After that little experience, whenever he saw a pig or a

The mugging of the shark.

flitch of bacon he used to go quite red in the face and everyone would laugh. But Robert was cured. He never kicked so much as a packet of pork scratchings ever again. The bit that Robert didn't like was being laughed at. Nobody likes to be laughed at and Robert least of all. He never said anything when people recalled the story of the stolen bacon butty and laughed, and they did it often. But he seethed inside and wondered how he could get his own back. It was about then that Robert realized that he didn't like people at all.

Then one day he read an article in a magazine about the lynching of a shark. 'Shark kills swimmer' is not a very unusual headline to see in the paper, but 'Swimmers lynch shark' really caught Robert's attention. This murder of a harmless shark happened somewhere in South Africa. A very handsome young life-saver had disappeared two days earlier. He was a very popular young man. He hadn't actually saved anyone's life but he looked good and lots of people took photographs of him. Anyway, he disappeared, and everyone said it was a shark that was responsible for Pedro Mamiya's disappearance. The bathers fumed as they got brown and talked endlessly

The butchers run off with the body.

about lovely Pedro who, incidentally, was a fisherman on the side. All of a sudden there was a great cry from near the water's edge: 'Great white shark!' All the people rushed down to the edge of the water. And there in the shallows, quite helpless, a great white shark floundered. It was a pitiful sight to see a fourteen-foot creature weighing nearly a ton flapping in fright in the shallow water. 'Remember Pedro,' went up the cry. And with that name all pity fled from the hearts of the holidaymakers. Women beat the poor creature with their handbags, and one drunken oaf chanted 'Here we go, here we go' as he peed in the shark's eye. And from somewhere, possibly Pedro's little wooden hut, several iron bars and machetes were produced. No matter that the great white shark is a protected species. Such was the ferocity of the sunbathers' attack that the entire body of the shark was cut into pieces. People were seen running away with shark parts. In certain parts of America a shark's jaw might fetch thousands of dollars. One crazed girl who had been out with Pedro the fisherman actually cut open the shark's stomach in the hope that Pedro might still be alive in there. After all, she thought, Jonah lived quite a long time

The school bullies don't know what Robert is plotting.

in the belly of a whale. It would have been a waste of breath to point out to her that a shark is a different kettle of fish. Anyway, she found no trace of Pedro, not even his badge. There was a Rolex watch in the stomach with 'R.M., *The Mirror*, Fleet Street' engraved on the back, which showed that the great white had done his duty elsewhere. But the Pedro-lovers had killed the wrong shark.

This slaughter of the innocent confirmed to Robert how awful people can be. And he hated them. He decided to throw in his lot with otters, sharks and stoats, with poisonous snakes and with rats, with cockroaches and spiders. The creatures that people hated and wanted to destroy Robert would love. He would love the hated and hate the people. But though he hated people he found that he had a brilliant way of hiding this hatred.

He decided to be very nice to everyone he met. And so well did he do this that nobody at all saw through his strategy. He was just so nice. At school his work was average-to-good, so that he was not a threat to the loud lads who were so influential in his group and who hated anybody they thought was clever. This goes on in lots of schools.

Young Robert spits in Nerys's cornflakes.

Plenty of clever children have to pretend to be not clever or else they get bullied by the thick. It's an odd thing about schools, they are supposed to teach you how to cope with life and yet they can't protect the gentle from thick bullies.

Robert was pleasant to all the girls he met casually at school or on the train. He even managed to convince Nerys that he was fond of her. He would quietly polish her best shoes when she was not there so that when she came to put them on she was delighted and felt that Robert was OK as a brother. She would have thought differently if she'd known that he used to spit in her cornflakes every morning.

And if Mrs Caligari needed something from the local supermarket Robert would always offer to go and fetch it. And so bit by bit people forgot about the pig-kicking days and just thought what a nice lad Robert was. It was a terrific achievement on his part. But though people forgot about Robert's little oddities, Robert never forgot his hatred of people. And behind his smiles raged the terrible thoughts of a miniature Richard the Third. 'I can smile, and murder while I smile.' It was Robert's favourite quote in all Shakespeare.

Robert thinks, 'Your number's up, Mr Grice.'

There was an old blind bachelor who lived in the village. He was a nice enough old boy who once upon a time used to play cribbage in the George and Dragon with Boris from Transylvania. He was a retired slaughterman. Milk lambs and sucking pigs had been his speciality, but he'd killed 139,000 calves too in his long career, though at home he wouldn't have hurt a fly. Everybody liked him. And this old boy's name was Frank Grice. He was so well loved that not even the midges used to bother him on warm summer evenings. It would have been a very rare creature indeed who would wish old Frank any harm. Robert Caligari was a very rare creature. And one Saturday morning as old Frank Grice was waiting to cross from just outside the Red Lion over to the Saxon Warrior, as the chemist's shop is called in Lenham, Robert saw his chance to avenge pigs, lambs and calves. It's a very busy crossing indeed, since the main square was closed off a few years ago. The locals called the corner Piccadilly Circus. Traffic approached it from four directions. People trying to get from the Saxon Warrior to the flower shop or from the bread shop to the car park or from the Red Lion to the post office had to watch out for their lives. So

Mr Grice on his way to heaven.

dangerous was it that sometimes the Air Ambulance was to be seen hovering overhead. The heavy lorries from local hauliers competed with invalid trolley and cyclists to negotiate the tricky corner.

Frank Grice was not afraid of the traffic. There was always someone there to guide him across. Robert saw old Frank waiting for someone to tell him when it was safe. The old boy had just had a couple of drinks, to judge from his breath. 'Final Selection' was his favourite tipple. Frank didn't know it but he had just had his final 'Final Selection'. A truck was coming down the High Street, too fast for safety. A beeping of a horn from someone who was parked badly outside the bread shop distracted people's attention for a split second. That was all the time Robert needed. With quite amazing cheerfulness he called out sweetly but clearly to old Mr Grice, 'All clear, Mr Grice.' The old man smiled for the last time as he thanked Robert for his kindness, and slipped him a pound for his trouble. And so Mr Grice stepped under the roaring TIR forty-tonner. The brakes shrieked as the driver did his best and hit the 'dead man's handle'. People screamed and rushed forward. Robert got there first. Looking under the truck, he

Robert plays the hypocrite.

saw with terrific pleasure that the old boy was a goner. And with tears of relief and glee he said to the thin man who ran the art gallery, 'Is he going to be all right, Mr Goode?' Mr Goode, a well-known amateur weightlifter, also looked under the lorry and promptly fainted. Robert prevented him from crashing to the ground and people were very touched at the boy's quick thinking. What they didn't see was that Robert managed to pick Mr Goode's pocket as he lay in a faint in the gutter.

The following Thursday Robert attended Mr Grice's funeral at St Mary's church. He even took a bunch of flowers, bought from the money he stole from his mother's purse, Nerys's pig Trevor and Mr Goode's pocket. He laid the flowers very reverently by the graveside and bowed his head. People noticed this profound respect from Robert and they nodded approvingly with tears in their eyes.

The pleasure Robert got from the death of old Mr Grice was so great that he thought he would faint. There is a certain pleasure that can make you quite breathless. Robert noticed that his hearing became more acute than before. When Nerys was eating her celery one evening Robert could hear her very clearly even though the TV

Nerys eats celery.

was on fairly loudly. He thought he could hear Mr Whiteside, the man next door, eating his celery too.

'I love celery,' murmured Nerys as she reached for her sixth stick.

'So does Mr Whiteside, by the sound of it,' muttered Robert.

'Mr Whiteside?' said Nerys. 'How do know that Mr Whiteside likes celery?'

'Because I can hear him,' said Robert. 'He's on his sixth stick, too . . . Oh, he's stopped now. No, he's started again.' Robert cocked his head like an attentive throstle. 'He's on radishes now,' he said, 'with salt on them.' This last little detail made Nerys laugh as she wiped a fragment of celery from her bumpy bottom lip.

Robert happened to be in the house by himself one day. His mother had taken Nerys to the doctor. Nerys wasn't feeling very well and her mum was rather worried. She would have been more worried if she had known that Robert had been putting tiny amounts of weedkiller in Nerys's porridge for the past few days. I mean really very tiny amounts, hardly visible to the naked eye, though obviously effective in the naked stomach of dreary old

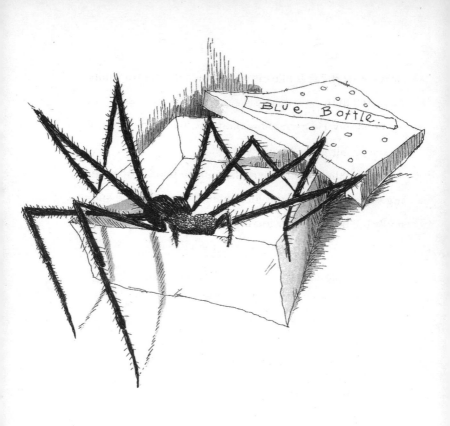

Bluebottle, the affectionate tarantula.

Nerys. Robert didn't like his sister much and he was quite pleased that the weedkiller was causing Nerys a bit of an upset tummy. He had always thought of her as weedy and therefore fair game to be poisoned.

Anyhow, there was Robert alone in the house and reading the small ads in the local paper when his eye suddenly fell on the following lines:

WANTED

Exchange a Tarantula Spider (in a box) for a snooker cue. The spider, Bluebottle by name, is in excellent condition and has been well looked after. The snooker cue would need to have been treated the same. Bluebottle is very affectionate if treated gently. He adores flies, so a dirty home would be preferable, though not essential. Apply in person to: Martyn, The Old Temperance Hall, 13a Meeting House Lane, Tovil, near Maidstone, Kent, bringing the snooker cue in its box, or call 0962 734 659. There will be a witness to the exchange should negotiations be concluded successfully.

This little ad intrigued Robert and he wondered if perhaps the man who was now tired of his tarantula might be persuaded to swap it for something other than a snooker cue.

Robert decided to call Martyn at The Old Temperance

Robert makes a sinister call to Martyn.

Hall and ask him a few questions about Bluebottle. He might even be able to persuade Martyn to meet him somewhere dangerous. Dangerous to Martyn, that is.

'Hello? Martyn speaking, how may I help you?' It sounded as if Martyn was under the bedclothes and the telephone in the next room.

Robert said: 'I have just seen your ad in the local paper and I was thinking that perhaps . . .'

'I don't know what you're talking about,' came the voice beneath the blankets.

Blankets? Maybe he's been buried alive and he's talking through four feet of earth, Robert said to himself. 'I wanted to talk to you about little Bluebottle,' he shouted down the phone.

'This is a very bad line,' came the muffled boom from The Old Temperance Hall. 'I can't hear you very clearly, are you the job centre?'

Robert looked out of the window to see if his mother and sister were coming along the road. No. All clear. He suddenly didn't like Martyn the muffler. 'No, this is the voice of doom,' he said.

Martyn suddenly sounded interested. There was a great

Robert is propositioned by Martyn.

deal of disturbance down near The Old Temperance Hall. Martyn was obviously either digging himself out of his bedclothes or clambering out of his grave. 'Did you say doom?' came the new voice of Martyn. 'Is this a joke or something?'

'It's no joke,' said Robert very coolly. 'I'm the voice of doom. It's my job to call people up and remind them that their number has come up.' Robert glanced at the clock above the picture of his uncle Bert. He said: 'It is now eleven-thirty and twenty seconds. In precisely three hours you are to die.'

There was a very interesting silence down the line. Not even the sound of breathing. Robert wondered if the shock of the news had already killed Martyn. He was a little irritated that Martyn seemed so uninterested in the news of his death in three hours time. 'Do you want to know any details while I'm on the line?' he asked. Silence. 'Hello,' called Robert. 'Are you still there?'

Silence for another few seconds and then Martyn said: 'That makes two of us, then, doesn't it? Do you want to come down to The Old Temperance Hall and we could die together? No one will know or mind,' he added. 'I'm

Sweet tea in the knife-box.

all alone down here. I could do with a friend to die with.'

Then he chuckled and Robert put the receiver down very gently. He sat there for a few moments and then got up and made himself a mug of tea. He was trembling slightly. The joke on Martyn at The Old Temperance Hall now seemed silly. And Martyn's chuckle had released in Robert the desire to do something to hurt someone.

While the kettle was coming to the boil Robert slipped into his leather jacket. Then he made the tea and gave himself two spoons of sugar. And as he lifted the cup he heard the sound of voices coming towards the house. His mother and Nerys were approaching. Very carefully Robert poured his tea into the knife-and-fork drawer and he quietly left the house by the back door. There was something he had to do.

About half a mile from Robert's house is the motorway, the M20. And about three hundred yards from the nearby motorway bridge was Robert's secret place. The great storms of 1987 had blown away hundreds of trees on the high ground above the motorway but some, though severely damaged, had survived. Robert's secret place was an old oak tree; its crown had been snapped

Robert's hideaway.

off in the great winds, but somehow the old tree had stayed upright, and it was in this shattered tree that Robert liked to pass the time and cultivate his hatred for the world. All he had were some old blankets, a few books by James Herbert, some cans of Coca Cola and his crossbow. There was also a big colour poster of Saddam Hussein, the ruthless dictator of Iraq, who was Robert's idol.

He sat in his tree, put on his radio as background comfort, and rocked back and forth, his eyes closed and his heart jumping. He was asking himself what he had to do and no answer was coming to him. No voice would whisper instructions to him. This absence of orders made Robert extremely uneasy. After a while he got up, and leaving his radio playing, he took his crossbow and one arrow and his kite, crept out of his tree and went along the high bank on the south side of the motorway. The large kite easily masked the deadly crossbow from the eyes of anyone who might pass.

He walked along the bank and waited for the voice to tell him what to do. But no instructions were relayed into Robert's brain this morning from the mysterious voice

Robert smiles as he plots.

that so often told him what was to be done. The voice that could not be disobeyed was not in his head.

About a few hundred yards from his tree he suddenly felt sick. His mouth filled with acid liquid and he was forced to spit it out while he waited for his stomach to stop heaving. Robert was quite used to being sick. He handled it very well and when he did throw up he always did so very neatly. He stopped and threw up. Immediately he felt better and could breathe easier and deeper.

He walked on for a few yards and then he sat down on an old tree stump and looked about him. The motorway was very busy. He noticed a lorry in the fast lane as it overtook other vehicles and he was reminded that it was forbidden for big lorries to do that. Curiously, Robert was quite strict in his views of how people should behave in cars. Whenever the whole family was in the car together going to Folkestone to see Auntie Wyn on a Sunday Robert would keep up a running commentary on the driving technique of all the drivers that passed them. 'Why don't you just shut up and give us a bit of peace, Robert?' his father would say. 'Yes, why don't you

Woman on a horse, 69 seconds before they die.

just shut up for ever?' Nerys would sometimes add. It was when she said such things that Robert would think of poisoning her. He sometimes thought about poisoning the whole world.

On the motorway bridge a woman on a horse was crossing. It was quite a peaceful sight to see, a creature going at such a slow pace on the bridge while the cars and trucks below raced as fast as they could get away with. As the horse and rider were crossing the bridge a tractor and trailer followed closely by a Toyota pick-up caused the woman on the horse to pull over. The tractor driver waved to the woman on the horse and passed her. The pick-up followed the tractor and then the voice in Robert's head said: 'Shoot the woman on the horse.'

Robert stretched like a cat deciding to go out and catch a nuthatch. The horse and rider were just over half-way across the bridge as Robert received his order to shoot the woman. The voice spoke again: 'Go on, get a move on or you'll be too late,' it said. The horse and rider were going towards Childwall Park and away from Robert. They were only about a hundred feet away from

A horse will fly and folk will die.

him. There were some berberis bushes between him and his target so he was pretty well screened. He raised his crossbow and took aim. The voice said: 'Shoot her in the bottom, that'll teach her.' Robert wanted to obey the secret voice. It was when the voice spoke and he was obeying that Robert felt most happy.

He looked down the sight at the swaying bottom of the horse topped by the swaying and swinging bottom of the woman. He always wanted to shoot women in the bottom. He squeezed the release and fired. As he fired he was just slightly distracted by a group of cyclists appearing on the bridge going in the same direction as Robert's swaying target. The arrow missed the top bottom and hit the lower bottom of the horse. The poor innocent creature reacted very badly. Sometimes horses are silly creatures. I have seen a horse rear up in a country lane as a rabbit ran in front of it. A rabbit, for God's sake! Anyway, the horse on Sandway bridge took the arrow in its arse to heart. It reared up as if it wanted to fly away. It was an amazing sight, with the arrow in its bottom. It looked like a nightmare unicorn. The woman clung on and did her best to calm the

Down, down, down went the innocent horse,
and death watched and waited.

shocked creature. The cyclists, heads down and legs whirling, went past the woman on the horse and they noticed nothing. The poor woman must have been very scared to be up there on a rearing horse and on a motorway bridge too. And she had reason to be scared. The horse leapt up and sideways and, trying to get away from the arrow in its arse, it jumped off the motorway bridge and fell down on to the south-bound carriageway below.

The screams from the terrified woman made Robert chortle with glee. He watched with utter delight as the poor horse and its terrified rider fell on to a coach carrying perhaps sixty senior citizens. The horse crashed through the roof and on to the driver, killing him instantly. The poor woman rider was still alive when she landed in the coach cab, still connected to the horse, but her escape was nothing more than a little respite. The coach swerved from the slow lane through the other two lanes and across the barrier. A petrol tanker coming the other way crashed straight into the coach, and the explosion that occurred would give Robert pleasure for another two minutes. The tanker overturned and there was a

Robert scarpers as all hell breaks loose.

volcanic eruption of flame. The escaped petrol ran like a stream along the motorway.

About twenty seconds later another petrol tanker crashed into the mangled and burning mass that just forty seconds ago had been a happy mobile theatre of pensioners all singing 'Cruising Down the River'. And as the whole area exploded into flames and smoke Robert turned, and clutching his kite and crossbow he ran towards his destiny.

As he raced back to his safe tree, to his asylum, Robert's heart was just singing; he was ecstatic, light as air and utterly happy. He felt like a gold-medal winner, the tops, the best, the very best. He was Robert the Gold, Robert the winner. Approaching his tree, he felt like an athlete nearing the tape. With one last supreme effort he quickened his stride as he neared the tangle of logs that lay in front of his shattered oak, his safe house, as they say in spy stories. As he took the last three yards at breakneck speed, he heard the sound of the radio in the tree, and he considered it a mistake. It might have given him away, he thought. But when you are as happy as Robert was at that moment you don't have a sense of

Robert falls head-first into his hideaway.

real time. Happiness scrambles all sense of time.

The parrot-like voice of a parrot-brained disc jockey was screeching out some banalities about the death of John Lennon. 'John Lennon? I'll bloody rock you faster than Lennon,' went one of the thoughts in Robert the Avenger's head. He should not have been listening. It was a terrible mistake. Somebody should tell the young how dangerous life is when they are happy. It's a state of mind that makes them feel like Superman, and we all know what happened to him.

Robert was as quick as a dragonfly. He was heavier, of course, but he was happy and so he forgot about the difference in weight; also, at full speed he didn't even see the seven crow turds in the middle of the rotten old log that was his bridge. 'Oh, shit,' he thought as he skidded on the crow turds, and his world turned upside-down.

He let the crossbow fall, and as if he was watching some crummy commercial about sky-divers and cottage cheese, he was aware that he had risen up and turned upside-down. For a split second all was still, and then he fell head-first into his fox hole, into his bolt hole, into his own grave.

Trapped and helpless in his den.

The great storm of 1987 had dealt very artistically with some of its victims. The shattering of old oaks had produced Big Bang effects inside the boles of ancient trees. The interior diameter of Robert's tree was about five feet, maybe a bit more. And within that old wooden cylinder the storm in its arrogant violence had redesigned things. At the base of the old oak were splinters like stalagmites, sharp as shrapnel and though beautiful to look at, terrifying to fall among. As Robert went down he raised his arms to save his face. He was not thinking, of course; the shift from happiness to terror was too quick for him to think. Down he went. He scarcely felt the opening of the flesh in the left side of his face or the blow to the point of his chin. Trying to protect his face and eyes, he twisted during that fall of thirteen feet. His right elbow was shattered as he landed and his left arm was rammed down between the stalagmites, which gripped him completely.

For just a tiny bit of time there was utter silence and a sort of peace. From joy to terror and shock to this strange silence. What now? thought Robert. And the answer came in a terrific wave of agony. The only true

Robert listens to Abba:

'Can You Hear the Bells, Fernando?'

pain Robert had ever felt before was the pain of his hatred for people, and in its strange way that had also been a pleasure. But not this pain, oh no. The agony was so amazing that for a while it threatened to carry him away with its force. But then it eased and the detail was dreadful. For a moment he thought he was swallowing sea water. Sea water in an oak tree? No. It was blood that was trickling down his throat from a wound in his mouth.

Robert wanted to say: 'Oh no, oh no.' But he couldn't speak. Why not? he wondered. And as he tried to control his tongue and shift the position of his head to avoid swallowing his own blood he realized that a piece of his tongue had gone – bitten off on the impact of his fall into the pit of his beloved old oak tree. His eyes rolled in their sockets and up towards his shattered elbow, and he caught sight of the missing fragment of his tongue gleaming like a piece of pig's liver on his jacket sleeve. A dreadful moan escaped him, a moan of despair like the groan of ancient plumbing in a very old house just before daylight. You know what I mean?

'What have I done to deserve this?' Robert wonders.

And the radio chattered on. It was someone's birthday. Robert groaned in the double agony of his injuries and his inability to smother the radio. It represented so much of the outside world he hated, the world that he had so often dreamed of destroying single-handed. Another wave of agony swept over him and he was suddenly aware that he felt sorry for the poor horse on the bridge. He wouldn't have deliberately hurt a horse. It was the woman astride it who was the target of his hatred. And as he was carried away into a sort of mist, while trying all the time not to swallow his blood, he felt a need to apologize to the unfortunate horse. Robert Caligari, who had never felt sorry for anything in his whole life, wanted to say sorry to a horse! Then darkness came over him.

As consciousness came back to him he was astounded to hear a high-pitched moaning. His eyes swivelled about to try and locate the source of the noise. And then he realized it was coming from within himself, from deep within himself. And the bloody radio was still talking away to his right. He had no idea how long he had been unconscious.

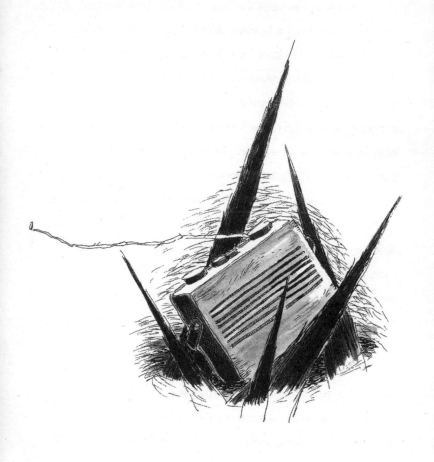

All the news that's fit to hear.

'The worst accident in the history of the motorways,' the radio was saying hysterically. 'It may be the worst accident ever, anywhere,' burbled the fatuous voice of the fatuous reporter. 'It appears that a woman lost control of a horse as she rode it across the Sandway motorway bridge. A nearby schoolteacher who was off school with flu and fiery sinuses saw the horse rear up and then jump to its left and over the bridge barrier and down on to the Ashford-bound traffic below. The horse fell on to a coach carrying sixty-nine elderly people on an outing to Notcutt's garden centre near the Bearstead crematorium, killing the driver immediately. The coach went out of control and crossed the central barrier and crashed head-on into a petrol tanker going in the opposite direction. The tanker, carrying a full load, burst into flames, as did the coach, and the whole area was covered in dense smoke. The teacher, a physics specialist who teaches near Grove Green, rushed to the bridge. So dense was the smoke and so fierce the heat he could not get on the bridge itself. The fire services were severely hampered by the smoke as well as by the police and the scores of people living nearby who rushed to help in any

Thirteen flaming vicars.

way they could. Eye-witnesses said they could only stand and watch in horror as a wave of blazing petrol swept along the motorway engulfing all in its path. Some people escaped from their burning cars and ran screaming up the bank of the motorway. One Volkswagen minibus carrying thirteen clergymen to a religious conference at Aylesford Friary was caught in the worst of the fiery flood. By a miracle all thirteen vicars managed to get out of the vehicle and were seen to run up the bank, every one of them ablaze.

"'It was awful," commented a passing tractor driver. "I'm not a religious man myself, live and let live, I say. But the sight of thirteen parsons all in flames was not a pretty one, believe you me. Pure Armageddon. And one of my mother's aunts was a nun, so I know what I'm talking about.'"

The newscaster shrieked out that he had located an off-duty colleague who happened to live near the scene. 'Can you hear me, Cassandra?' screeched the anchorman in the studio.

'Yes, David,' squawked Cassandra, 'I'm getting you hot and strong.'

Cassandra the half-witted reporter.

'What's it like there, Cassandra?' asked David.

'Well, David,' said Cassandra, 'it's difficult to describe.'

'Why is that, Cassandra?' asked daft David.

'Well, for one thing, there's an awful lot of smoke here,' gasped Cassandra.

'Don't tell me they are allowing *smoking* at the scene of an accident,' wailed David the brain, as he was called by the canteen staff.

'No, David, it's just that . . .' There was a pause and various mutters. Cassandra then came on strong and full of passion. 'David, I have just been handed a piece of paper by a witness who lives around here and who has been witnessing the sights for some time.'

'Read it out, Cassandra,' ordered the brain in the studio.

And then Cassandra came on the hot air with a great announcement. 'David, I am now going to read out the report from our witness. "There is a river of blazing petrol rolling back towards Maidstone. Many approaching cars were going too fast and were instantly swallowed up in the flames. Many cars stopped in time and their occupants scrambled up the embankment to safety."'

Darby and Joan in their beloved old Morris Minor.

'Any special incidents?' asked David of Cassandra. 'I mean, any names or acts of heroism for our listeners? Any particular horrors?'

'Yes, David, yes indeed there are. I mean there have been.'

'Well, Cassandra, well?' asked David.

'Well, David,' cried Cassandra, 'an extraordinary incident took place only a few hundred yards from where I am standing with my witness. It appears that an old bull-nosed but immaculate Morris Minor was stopped by several brave people who had abandoned their own cars and were trying to warn oncoming drivers about the tidal wave of petrol that was approaching. It appears that the elderly couple inside the old Morris did not want to leave their beloved old vehicle. And David, I'm quoting now, the old couple said: "This car has been a good and loyal servant to us for nearly fifty years. A friend. It has never let us down once and we are certainly not going to leave it in its hour of need." And David,' continued Cassandra, 'you are not going to believe this. Are you ready, David?'

'I'm ready, Cassy,' sobbed David. 'We're all ready, Cassy,

Snap! The last picture.

don't spare us any details, the heart has its reasons.'

'Well, David, it seems that one of the rescuers, a Mr Ted Crump, spoke for the whole group. He said to the old lady and gentleman: "But it's only an old car, and life is sweet and you only get one bite of the cherry, so leave it and live."' Cassandra drew breath and went on: 'But it was all to no avail, David. The seven good Samaritans had to leave the elderly couple as the river of flame swept towards them. And Mr Crump told me, David, that as he looked back towards that dear old couple from the safety of the embankment he could see the two old people waving. Waving, David. And not only waving, but waving cheerfully, too, from the cockpit of their beloved old car, which was more precious to them than anything else and without which life was not worth living. And a split second before the old bull-nose was engulfed, Mr Crump noticed that the old lady was taking a picture of him with her Canon Sureshot, and asking him, in the manner of Hylda Baker, to *smile*! Mr Crump, Reg to his friends, said that he smiled as best he could, but in spite of the heat it was not a warm smile, he said.'

A Mercedes-Benz grilled to a cinder.

And so the news of these horrors continued, as for nearly three-quarters of a mile the burning fuel swept back along the lines of stranded cars. It consumed them with effortless confidence and utter indifference as to model. At one moment, as the flames swallowed a tasty-looking Mercedes-Benz carrying Belgian number plates, it seemed as if a nearby Robin Reliant which had scuttled to the hard shoulder and mounted the bank might escape. Cassandra, whose voice now sounded almost interesting now that it had all but disappeared, painted the picture of the fate of the Robin Reliant with all the tiny passion of which she was capable. Her voice was so hoarse that the absence of sincerity was hidden from the listeners.

'David,' she husked, 'you are not going to believe this.' Cassandra always prefaced anything she said with this phrase.

And David said, as usual: 'Try me, Cassy, try me.'

'Well, David,' said Cassandra, 'for a moment it looked as if one small little car might escape the cruel flames. It was a little Robin Reliant. You know?'

'I know, Cassy,' yelped David. 'Oh, I know very well

A brave little Robin Reliant.

what you mean. My Auntie Gladys and Uncle Fred had a Robin Reliant. They practically lived in it. During the summer, I mean. I never did find out what happened to that dear little car. But go on, Cassandra, you were talking about a Robin Reliant.'

'Oh, so I was,' said Cassandra, who had quite forgotten what she was talking about. With a terrific effort of concentration she took up the story. 'Well, David, it seems that this little Robin Reliant, just like the one your Uncle Fred used to live in, drew up on the hard shoulder and tried to mount the bank. For a moment it looked as if it might hold its position. Several people, led by Mr Ted Crump who was just everywhere, tried to hold on to the little car and kept up a non-stop stream of encouragement to the driver. They all struggled for nearly eight minutes before they lost their grip and the poor little thing rolled back down the embankment and into the waiting flames.'

'Oh, my God!' groaned David, moved to something like emotion. 'Oh, my God, Cassy. Oh, my God! And then?'

Cassandra was quick on her cue this time. 'Well, David,

Ebb and Flo on their way to a party.

it just seemed like fate. I suppose you could say that their number was up.'

'Was there anyone in the cab?' asked David, revealing again that there was not much inside his cab.

Cassandra pushed on. 'Well, David, it seems that there were two people in the car, a man accompanied by another man. They were twins, both of them. Twin brothers. At least that's what they told Mr Crump, who is very good on details and picked all this up while trying to save the little car. Both the men were of male sex and aged seventy-three. It would appear that they were on their way to the birthday party of their old headmaster, but as I say, their number was up. Their name was on the bullet.'

'Oh, my God!' responded David the brain, who would have said the same thing if Cassandra had told him it was raining.

'We rang the old headmaster,' said Cassandra, 'to tell him of the tragedy and to spoil his party.'

'Oh, my God!' groaned David. 'And what did he say?'

'Well, David, it seems he was too upset to talk coherently. All he kept saying was the twins were good at geography and nothing like this had ever happened before.

David the prat babbles to Cassandra.

He said that they were very well behaved and also liked sailing.'

'Oh, my God!' cried David, dry eyed. 'And did you find out anything else that our listeners might like to hear?'

'How do you mean, David?' asked Cassandra.

'Well, Cassandra,' replied David, picking up on Cassandra's speech patterns, 'did they have any birthmarks, for example, or indeed any identifying details?'

Cassandra seemed to be thinking. 'Well, David, the headmaster just kept repeating through his tears that the twins were good boys and liked sailing. He also mentioned that their nicknames were Ebb and Flo.'

'Oh, my God!' gasped David. 'Ebb and Flo?'

Robert Caligari heard all this with amazing clarity. And the clearer the sound was, the greater his own agony. And so the mayhem caused by Robert's hatred of people grew and grew.

Two television crews were on their way to Ashford to report on a small fire behind the Marks and Spencer branch there. They were men of the world, those two crews – been in the Lebanon they had, and in the Gulf. And they hurtled towards what they thought was Marks

The roasting of the cocks.

and Sparks. Then it was just sparks as they ran into the stream of flames that immediately engulfed them, and as they perished they must have wondered why they hadn't stayed in the Middle East.

Just behind the doomed TV crew, and as if to prove that truth is stranger than fiction, came a lorry carrying six thousand chickens and three hundred cockerels to a poultry farm near Wormshill. The tyres of the lorry melted immediately and the vehicle ground to a halt as though in sand. How the cocks crowed, even though the dawn was past. And on the other side of the motorway, a van carrying three thousand bottles of red wine exploded and the wine cascaded down on the roasting poultry. Within minutes the smell of *coq au vin* could be sniffed all over the district. The schoolmaster on the bridge who was watching all this horror and had three chickens of his own wept openly.

By now all television and radio networks were carrying the story.

A very old lady who lived about four hundred and fifty yards away from the disaster happened to be watching

A nearby nosy parker spots a dancing fiddler.

the spot where the poor horse had jumped from the motorway bridge. She had a very powerful pair of binoculars, inherited from her father, who had been a rear admiral and who had retired to Pluckley where he had been happy with the ghosts of so many other ex-admirals. She had never married but was incredibly curious about what went on within the range of her binoculars. She called the local police and reported that she had seen what she could only describe as a boy running away from the scene. She said he seemed to be dancing as he went and appeared also to be carrying a kite and a violin perhaps.

Instantly all the hacks reporting on the horror began to claim that the horse had been frightened by a hooligan carrying a kite or by the same hooligan playing the fiddle on Sandway bridge. Perhaps he was a disenchanted morris dancer, they speculated. The local paper announced that it would give a substantial reward for information leading to the arrest of the kite-carrier who also played the violin.

In the oak tree this piece of news was relayed to Robert as he emerged from another period of uncon-

The crow that felled Robert with seven fatal plops.

sciousness. For a few moments the description of a dancing boy tangoing away from the bridge and carrying a violin made him forget his agony. But as the figure of 'more than two hundred deaths are feared' was reported, his pain came back with a rush and he wished he had stuck to the slow poisoning of his sister Nerys. Too late now.

He looked up and saw a large crow watching him from the entrance to his safe hole. It was the same crow which had dropped the seven deadly turds on the log on which he had skidded. The crow was without remorse.

Robert's safe hole! He was safe now, he thought. As safe as houses. And the irony hit him. As safe as houses! And he suddenly remembered how as a child he had enjoyed kicking his sister's piggy bank. That was what had got him started as a pig-kicker. And then the pain came and so bad was it and so shocking to Robert's system that he slipped into the comforting state of semi-consciousness.

And on the motorway with all approaching traffic stopped there was the biggest traffic jam in the history

Motorway carnage.

of the system. Helicopters flew over the scene of the tragedy and reporters competed in their hysteria to describe the scene.

'It is so awful, Hilary,' said the ITN man, 'that it is inde-scribable. Words cannot do it justice.' So he was no use to anybody at all. Later he was given an OBE for his con-tribution to broadcasting. He then took early retirement and started to learn the violin.

The local hospitals were all on full alert and their emergency procedures were tested to the limit. Teams of counsellors were flown in from Liverpool and Notting-ham to comfort the fraught. The burns units in all hospi-tals within a range of twenty-five miles clicked into operation. Special telephone numbers were given out on all radio and TV stations so that anxious parents and rel-atives could get news of their burnt ones.

And as the afternoon drew to a close the dreadful agony of Robert Caligari went on in the storm-blasted oak tree. The figures of dead and injured were put out at nearly three hundred. There were constant references to the smell of burning chicken and boys who played the violin. Further back along the road a farm truck full of

The old boys in the Red Lion enjoy the bad news.

pigs for slaughter had been caught in the inferno, and the overpowering smell of roast pork could be nosed from as far away as Hollingbourne in the Maidstone direction to Charing Heath in the direction of Ashford. A huge French lorry carrying ninety tonnes of cabbages from Lille in northern France to Nine Elms, London, was also caught in the sudden motorway hell, the like of which even Frenchmen had never seen. Add the smell of roasting pork to that of roasted chicken and then add on the stench of burnt cabbage and you can understand why so many vegetarians for miles around were feeling sick.

The catastrophe was the sole subject of talk in all the pubs and working men's clubs everywhere. Her Majesty sent word of her sympathy and in number 7A, Vampire Close, Lenham, Mrs Caligari began to be worried about her son Robert.

As Robert had no friends that she could remember her anxiety grew as midnight approached. At twelve sharp she called the local police and reported her son missing. Mrs Caligari was stunned when the policeman who took her call asked her if Robert was a dancer or played the

'Does your son dance or play the violin?'

asked the policeman.

violin. 'Not as far as I know,' she told the prying copper, 'he's very much a boy who keeps himself to himself, so I don't suppose he'd like dancing.' 'But would you say he was light on his feet?' pursued the ardent constable. Mrs Caligari said that yes, Robert was very light on his feet and so was his sister Nerys when her stomach was not playing her up.

The policeman thanked her and said they would be in touch if they heard anything about her son. This report was filed along with the earlier message from the old lady with the powerful binoculars who had told the local law that she had seen a boy dancing across the field away from the motorway bridge where the horse had jumped over the barrier on to the traffic below.

And in his oak tree, when he was conscious, Robert could just hear the noise of the rescue workers only a few hundred yards from where he lay so hopelessly trapped.

As the bells of St Mary's church tolled Robert the time, some sixth sense told him that he was being looked at. His mouth was so swollen he couldn't keep

Hello, little rat. What do you want?

it closed, and his moans of pain were quite involuntary. But this feeling that someone or something was near him in his tree gave him the self-control to hold in his moans and listen and look. This was not easy, as the wound to the side of his face seemed to have made his neck so stiff he could hardly move it. But he managed to turn his head and widen his angle of view to his left. Nothing. He wondered if Martyn from The Old Temperance Hall in Meeting House Lane might by some miracle be there with his tarantula spider, Bluebottle.

He raised his eyes towards the entrance above him, where the moonlight came in. And there on the shattered rim of Robert's magic oak, clear as a tiny monument in the moody light of the moon, sat a rat. A large rat with bright, fearless eyes.

Robert looked up at the rat and thought how wonderful it looked, all backlit by the moon. The rat was one of Robert's favourite creatures. He had for so long admired the intelligence of rats, and also their tenacity and bravery. Robert had often wished he had been born a rat himself. When a rat really wants something

The friendly rat peeps down Robert's leg.

he usually gets it. And Robert wondered what the rat wanted.

The rat sat up straight and seemed to take a deep breath. Then it made its way down the inside of the old oak, treading with marvellous care and perfect confidence as if it had lived in the old tree all its life. Robert's left leg was raised up towards the rat, which stopped and looked with curiosity at Robert's muddy trainer. And then without as much as a by-your-leave the rat nimbly climbed over Robert's foot and slithered inside the leg of his jeans and began to walk with infinite care down Robert's leg. Fear and revulsion caused Robert's whole body to convulse. The movement brought back the pain again and made his head swim and unconsciousness called him. But the thought of the rat down his trouser leg kept Robert aware. He felt it move inside his jeans. And then with terrific relief he felt it move back towards his foot and he watched it emerge blinking, as if it had just come out of the cinema, onto his trainer.

For a moment the rat seemed hesitant. It looked up towards the moonlight streaming into the tree. It

'Hello,' said the rat. 'Have I got news for you!'

made a small movement as if to go up and out when a loud moan from Robert caused it to stop and turn. It looked at Robert and seemed to remember why it was there. And then as if to tell Robert all about its intentions it ran swiftly along Robert's leg, over his stomach and up his chest and stopped with its back legs on Robert's throat and its front paws on Robert's chin. And then it dawned on Robert that the rat had come for him. Because Robert could only look with difficulty down his nose, and because it was so close and therefore out of focus, the rat now seemed to be enormous. It seemed very interested in Robert and leaned forward as if to introduce itself and looked right into his left eye.

Robert managed to push air through his swollen lips and for an instant the hiss and gurgle from Robert's mouth made the rat uncertain. Robert repeated his painful outbreathing to drive the rat away. And the rat was fascinated by the little puffs of air that came from the ripe, swollen lips of the helpless boy. It raised itself up a little and moved left and up again and then, as friendly creatures often do, it touched

Robert gives the rat some lip.

Robert's nose with its nose. Robert felt the exquisite, delicate movements of the rat as it moved up further and looked left into Robert's right eye. And suddenly Robert knew for certain what the rat wanted: it wanted *him*! His heart banged in his chest like the sound of a desperate prisoner hammering on a dungeon door. His groans sounded like the struggle for breath of a creature in quicksand. And from a throaty, low, hoarse growl Robert cried out as the rat bit the end of his nose.

The cry startled the rat and irritated it too. The rat slithered down an inch or two and in revenge for being disturbed it bit deeply into Robert's lower lip. The final nightmare of Robert Caligari had begun. The rat now set about the lips of the boy as if there was a strict time limit, as if it was in a competition. It stripped the top lip back as far as the gums, then it went lower to the bottom lip and one of its front feet slipped into Robert's mouth. The engorged remnant of his tongue prevented him from closing what remained of his lips. But so great was his terror that with a supreme and agonizing effort he managed to

Robert bites back. It was a bad mistake.

clench its teeth and bit the rat's front foot. But Robert was too weak to hold on, and with a squeal the rat snatched his foot free. It stood up straight and looked at Robert in amazement. So close was it now that Robert thought it to be three feet long. And perhaps it was his fear but Robert thought the rat cleared its throat. It looked him in the eye as if to say, 'You should not have done that, Robert, my son.' It bobbed down again and, moving its front feet carefully, resumed its feast on the tip of Robert's nose.

So great was the horror that Robert felt his thoughts runnning wildly through his brain as if they themselves were trying to think of an escape route, anything rather than endure this pain. He imagined the pleasure of being shot between the eyes by a cold, merciless assassin. Yes, that would be a relief, said the thought as it flashed through his brain. Then another thought offered itself, of his throat being cut. Yes! Yes! Yes! agreed the demented Robert, anything but this. Not to be eaten by a rat.

But there was to be no comfort or mercy for the boy who had never shown mercy to his victims in the days when he was strong and when his cunning had made

Two rats meet in the moonlight. Grief for Robert.

him the master of innocent creatures. His pain and terror were now so great that Robert could imagine nothing worse. As this thought came to him the rat stopped chewing at Robert's nose. It raised itself again and sniffed very clearly and twitched its whiskers. And then suddenly it sat up and froze. How beautiful it looked with the moonlight streaming down on its blood-soaked whiskers!

But what had caused the rat alarm? There was a little, little squeak from over the rim of the blasted tree and into sight, lit by the smoky moon, came another rat! A smaller rat. With amazing confidence it made its way towards the first rat and crouched low before it, as if bowing in respect. The first rat leaned forward and down and they touched noses. The second rat seemed a bit shy and turned its head to one side. Then the first rat leaned closer and seemed to whisper something in the shy rat's ear. A proposition, perhaps? The shy one considered the proposition and seemed suddenly pleased with whatever had been suggested. And moving forward and round it crouched side by side with the master rat. The smallest squeak came from the big

Beauty is in the eye of the beholder.

one and then exactly in step, as if in rodent dressage, the two rats came over Robert's face and looked at him closely, one rat in each eye.

The tears ran down what was left of Robert's face and he could feel the big rat and his new girlfriend paddling in them and he could hear little squeaks of pleasure from the two rats as they set about enjoying their first dinner date as an item. So great was their pleasure that their droppings fell freely and plentifully into Robert's mouth. The new rat took a big bite from the lower lip but didn't seem to like what she tasted. Could anything be worse than this?

Oh, yes, there was one more agony to come. One more agony even worse than anything that had happened before. Again the two rats were side by side, facing their first meal as a couple. Robert closed his eyes. And as he felt the rats' teeth slice through his eyelids he wished he had never been born. And as the rats settled down to their dessert of salted eye jelly, madness settled down on Robert Caligari. And soon came the darkness. And at last it was over.

And as for the rats? Well, as far as I know they lived

happily ever after and had lots of babies. And when they grew up they all came to the hollow oak and had a bite at what remained of the boy who kicked pigs, hated people and wished that he had been born a rat.

'Goodnight, Robert,' squeaked the rats.
'Thanks for the meal!'